Samuel French Acting Edition

Brontë

A Solo Portrait of Charlotte Brontë

by William Luce

SAMUELFRENCH.COM   SAMUELFRENCH.CO.UK

FOR PRODUCTION ENQUIRIES

UNITED STATES AND CANADA
Info@SamuelFrench.com
1-866-598-8449

UNITED KINGDOM AND EUROPE
Plays@SamuelFrench.co.uk
020-7255-4302

Each title is subject to availability from Samuel French, depending upon country of performance. Please be aware that *BRONTË* may not be licensed by Samuel French in your territory. Professional and amateur producers should contact the nearest Samuel French office or licensing partner to verify availability.

MARINES MEMORIAL THEATRE
A TRADITION IN QUALITY ENTERTAINMENT
609 SUTTER AT MASON · SAN FRANCISCO
UNDER THE GENERAL DIRECTION OF CHARLES H. DUGGAN

CHARLES H. DUGGAN

presents

JULIE HARRIS

in

BRONTË

A Solo Portrait of Charlotte Brontë

Written by

WILLIAM LUCE

Production Stage Manager
Kim O'Bannon

Executive Producers
Cheryl L. Fluehr
Joe R. Watson

Directed by

CHARLES NELSON REILLY

Produced by special arrangement with
EIS Presentations / Joan Simmons
& Bill Dyer

To Mother

PREFACE

I first wrote *Brontë* as a radio play for actress Julie Harris to perform on WGBH's *Masterpiece Radio Theatre*, Elinor Stout directing. The play was titled *Currer Bell, Esq.* (Charlotte Brontë's *nom de plume.*) This production won the Peabody Award, the Ohio State Award and Columbia University's Armstrong Award. It was subsequently recorded by Caedmon Records under the direction of Ward Botsford.

Brontë then became a movie. Producer Sonny Fox took it to Ireland, where it was filmed by Irish Television in County Wicklow. Again, Julie Harris starred, with Delbert Mann directing.

I then turned *Brontë* into a stage play. During her long commitment to a television series, Miss Harris tried out the play at several benefits, with Kristoffer Tabori directing. Later, under the sponsorship of producers Joan Simmons and Bill Dyer, Miss Harris performed Brontë at many colleges, universities and theaters. With Charles Nelson Reilly as director, *Brontë* formally opened at Charles Duggan's Marines Memorial Theatre in San Francisco in January, 1988.

Charlotte Brontë was born on April 21, 1816. She lived and wrote in the isolated moorland village of Haworth in the Yorkshire West Riding. With "Currer Bell" as her pen name, her sisters, Emily and Anne, took the names of Ellis Bell and Acton Bell, respectively. "We did not like to declare ourselves women," Charlotte later explained, "because we had a vague impression that authoresses are liable to be looked on with prejudice."

Charlotte's novel, *Jane Eyre*, was published in 1847. It was a tremendous success. Emily's *Wuthering Heights* and Anne's *Agnes Grey* followed soon after.

The secret of their literary genius undoubtedly lay in their childhood. With their equally talented brother, Branwell, the girls played at being writers. In microscopic handwriting, the four children penned romances, poems, and dramas, illustrating them with Arabian Nights pictures of fairy realms. It was a game which, for Charlotte, Emily and Anne in adulthood, became the serious business of writing.

Based on her writings and correspondence, *Brontë* begins in 1849 with Charlotte, at thirty-three, returning from Scarborough, where she has buried Anne. Branwell and Emily have died within the last year. Only Charlotte and her stern, God-fearing father are left in this house of memories. "I am certainly doomed to be an old maid," Charlotte has confided to friend Ellen Nussey. It would now seem that her fears are being realized.

As the play unfolds, Charlotte comes to terms with her genius and her need for love. To Ellen she writes, "To sit in a lonely room—the clock ticking loud through a still house—and have opened before the mind's eye the record of the last year, with its shocks, sufferings, losses—is a trial. Sometimes, Nell, I have a heavy heart of it. *But I am not crushed.*"

Welcome to Haworth.

William Luce
June, 1988

CHARACTERS

Charlotte Brontë

SETTING

The parlor in the Parsonage of St. Michael
and All Angels Church in the village of Haworth,
in the high moor country of Yorkshire, England.

The time is June 21, 1849

BRONTË

ACT I

(At RISE: We hear thunder and wind, gusting and wild. Occasional flashes of lightning are seen. From stage right CHARLOTTE BRONTË enters. She wears a cloak and bonnet. She calls to offstage, as she appears with carrying case.)

CHARLOTTE. Thank you, no, Mister Nicholls. I'll carry it in myself. Good-day! *(To audience:)* When Mister Arthur Bell Nicholls is at the reins, the horse takes its own sweet time. But what a beautiful rainbow there was! *(As NICHOLLS:)* Rainbow? What rainbow? *(To audience:)* "That rainbow!" says I. Poor, dear Mister Nicholls. *(Calling offstage to housekeeper, MARTHA:)* Never mind, Martha, I'm already in. *(To audience:)* Glory, Martha must have left every window in the house open. *(To MARTHA:)* Martha, close the windows upstairs. *(To audience:)* What wretched weather. The first day of summer it is, and yet the afternoon set in so fitful and cold.

There is something so merciless in the heavy rush of the wind across the moors. It wakens feelings in me I can't satisfy. A thousand wishes rise at its call, and they will die with me, never fulfilled. Then rushing impetuously upon me like the wind, comes a mighty phantasm of images conjured from nothing into a system strong as any religious creed. It acts upon me like opium, coiling about me, a disturbing but fascinating spell. And I know then that I, Charlotte Brontë, can write—*(Long pause.)*—*gloriously.*

(She removes her cloak and examines it.)

The ride from Keighley seemed endless. Mister Nicholls met me there at the station, and I was in no condition to be met by anyone. Now just look at this. My good cloak, ruined.

On the train to Leeds, a little girl and her mother sat opposite me. They hadn't been there for a full minute, before without any warning or the slightest indication of nausea, sickness overcame her, and the curdled contents of her little stomach, consisting apparently of a milk breakfast, were unceremoniously deposited in my lap. What a pretty mess. And to add insult to injury, the mother accused *me* of being the cause. She said I scowled at the child when they sat down, and made her little darling feel unwelcome.

Well, with water and a towel I managed to make myself presentable. Presentable, that is, to those lacking olfactory organs. *(Sniffing at the cloak.)* I'm afraid it's turning sour. *(Rubbing it.)* I'm sure Mister Nicholls noticed. He walked three feet ahead of me all the way to the gig. I could hardly keep up with him.

I speak of Papa's assistant curate. He's Irish, like Papa. The Reverend Arthur Bell Nicholls. Sometime back, there was idle talk going around that Mister Nicholls and I were going to marry. Imagine. A clerical romance. Well, it wasn't true, but I was grateful for the rumor.

(She hangs up cloak.)

Now where the deuce is my umbrella? I suppose Nell picked it up at the station by mistake. We parted so suddenly.

(She goes to the hearth, taking up the bellows, attempting to revive the fire.)

Botheration! The peat must be damp. *(To TABBY offstage:)* Tabby! *(To audience:)* She probably can't hear me, she's so deaf. *(Calling again:)* Tabby? *(To audience:)* We need some dry, that's what we need.

(She crosses to the cabinet and collects ink well, quill and paper. She goes to the large table and sits. She puts on her spectacles and starts to write a letter.)

(To NELL, writing:) To Ellen Nussey, Brookroyd, West Riding, Yorkshire. Twenty-first of June, 1849. Dear Nell, I got home a little before eight o'clock. The sky was black, but there was the most beautiful rainbow over the moors. All was clean and bright waiting for me. The dogs seemed in a strange ecstasy. I'm certain they regarded me as the harbinger of others.

(She removes her spectacles, rises, and continues the letter in her mind.)

There's a sense of desolation here, of agony to be undergone, as I resume life in this lonely house with Papa as my sole companion.

Why does anyone come back to Haworth? Why do I? It's almost July, and not one flower. Only the same gritstone hill

where the moors begin, Papa's church and the old stone
Parsonage with those two ugly thorn trees in front. A perfect
misanthrope's heaven, my sister Emily used to call Haworth.
Such a dirty, cramped little town. Well, cleanliness may be next
to godliness in the Bible, but in Haworth it's next to impossible.

*(She sits down again at the table, puts on her spectacles and
    resumes her letter to NELL.)*

(To NELL, writing:) I confess, Nell, I'm inclined towards
esteem and affection for Mister Nicholls. And I think something is brewing in his mind. At the gate, he asked if he might
call at the Parsonage tonight. Mind you, he's made no decla-
ration of his feelings for me, so I have no reason, really, to
hope. But he did look at me rather fervently, as if he wanted to
say something, but was shy. I wonder. I trust in Heaven that
Papa won't be hostile should my intuition be true.

*(She is interrupted by the sound of the front door knocker. For
    a moment, she is transfixed. She removes her spectacles,
    stands and steps toward the hallway door.)*

It couldn't be Mister Nicholls already. *(To MARTHA offstage:)* Martha? Would you see to the door?

(Sharply to dog:) Flossie, stop you barking! *(To audience
after pause:)* It's not Mister Nicholls. Almost every day, late
into the evening, we're assailed by strangers. They come bor-
ing into Haworth on the wise errand of seeing the author of
"Jane Eyre." God deliver me from my admirers.

So it's home again. I call it home still, much as London
would be called London, if an earthquake shook its streets to
ruins.

(She sits on the settee.)

The past months have gone by darkly and heavily, like a funeral train. Since September last, sickness has not quitted this house. It seems death is never far from us.

Well, do you wonder? Look at us, surrounded on three sides by a landscape of tombstones. Here, here and here. And inside Papa's church it's even worse.

On his last official visit to Haworth, Mister Benjamin Herschel Babbage, the government inspector, said quite emphatically that no further burials should take place under the church aisle. His speech was memorable ...

(She stands and steps downstage, now imitating the bumptious official.)

(As BABBAGE.) The exhalations and noxious gases exuding from the decaying remains of past generations that are laid to rest under the aisle of Saint Michael and All Angels, not to mention the permanent placement of large slabs of stone as grave covers, which prevent the access of atmospheric zephyrs to the ground, a condition necessary for the desired decomposition of dead bodies, have long rendered this house of God an impossible place in which to worship, without the swooning supplicant being pungently reminded of the ultimate end of all things.

(To audience:) Oh, Mister Benjamin Herschel Babbage, how right you are. *(Tapping foot on floor.)* Mister Babbage once told me that Papa's church is the only one he knows that has a full congregation when empty.

My sister Anne is the only family member not interred under the cold damp stone floor across the way. It's from Scarborough that I've just returned, where I buried Anne this four weeks past. It was my decision to lay the flower in the place where it fell. I have no preference for place. And there's little pleasure in kneeling in Papa's church, knowing that your nearest and dearest are moldering directly under your knees.

(She steps to the rocker, tea tray beside, and lifts the tea cosy.)

I'm exhausted with this whole business of dying. *(Pause.)* I hate this teapot.

(She steps to the fireplace to warm herself.)

And funerals, dear God, I'm worn out with them. I'm tired of having to be staunch and unafraid, because I *am* afraid. And I refuse to wear black anymore.

Tabby is upset for my not having brought Anne back home to Haworth, to rest under the church aisle with the others. Tabby thinks we should all be buried together, so that on the Final Day of Resurrection, we won't lose each other in all the confusion.

You see, toward the end, my sister begged to visit Scarborough, because of her happy memories there as a governess. Papa knew it would be disastrous for one so far advanced in the consumptive way. But she pleaded so pitifully, that he finally relented and let me take her—my friend Nell and me. That was a month ago. Anne was only twenty-nine.

I shall always remember her as she was that last evening— sitting by the window, looking out to sea. Such tranquility in her face.

(Conversing in memory.) Anne, what are you thinking of? *(To audience:)* "Of the next existence," she said simply. Oh, no, please.

But Anne was lost in her dreams. The most glorious sunset illumined the sky. The castle on the cliff was gilded in light. The little boats near the beach heaved on the tide, glittering like burnished gold. Anne seemed almost—well, almost transfigured. But her strength was fled. And so she died. She went so gently, we hardly realized. I think she knew it would be easier, the letting go—by the sea.

(Looking for spectacles:) Where are those damned spectacles?

(She stands and crosses, finding the spectacles in her purse.)

I dislike these. I think they look hideous. They leave a cleft right here. *(Touching bridge of her nose.)* Papa has one.

(She sits at the table again, puts on her spectacles and resumes her letter to NELL.)

(Writing.) I'm trying to be glad I've come home, Nell. I've always felt happy before, but this time, joy isn't the sensation. I feel the house in all its silence, the rooms all empty, where eight short months ago we were all together—Emily, Anne and our brother Branwell.

(She moves away from the table, removing her spectacles.)

(To audience.) In this room, my sisters and I used to assemble after supper, the dishes done, and walk and talk and read aloud our day's writings. We did, Emily, Anne and I. We

called it "perambulating."

(She strides around the table happily.)

We perambulated arm-in-arm this way, like restless, wild animals, around and around the table, after everyone had gone to bed. It was here I first heard "Wuthering Heights," chapter by chapter. Emily read it to us, night after night. Afterwards, I couldn't sleep, it was so vivid and fearful, every page charged with a sort of electricity. Brooding and dark, as if hewn in some wild workshop.

(She sits on the settee with a book.)

Even today when I read "Wuthering Heights," it's like breathing lightning. *(Pause.)* Oh, Emily, gone like a dream.

(She resumes the letter to NELL in her mind.)

Actually, Nell, I love Memory tonight. I prize her as my best friend. She gives me a deep delight. The hours, the thoughts, the hopes of my youth. Vast and sweet they seem now. They cling to every smallest corner of this gray stone house ...

(She goes to the cabinet and looks at the shelves.)

... to the long-locked drawers and shelves. And to this cupboard shut up for years, filled with tokens of childhood. *(Opening cabinet door.)* Oh, here are my brother's toy soldiers. *(Removing them.)* Papa purchased them in Leeds years ago for Brany. I remember the morning he brought them home. There was such excitement when they marched into the Parsonage.

Brany gave Waiting Boy to Anne. He waits. And Gravey to Emily. Brany took Sergeant Bud and Bonaparte, and mine was the Duke of Wellington. Duke for short.

(She plays a make-believe game with the soldiers.)

The Duke says, "How goes the watch, sir?"
What watch, Dukie?" says Gravey. *(Hiccup.)*
"You're drunk!" says the Duke. "You'll face a court-martial for this, sir!"
Brump, brump, brump.
"Ready, aim, fire!"

(She removes several tiny books from the cabinet.)

Those games led to our tiny books. We wrote these as children. The tales of Angria and Gondal and the great Glasstown adventures. Brany called it our "scribblemania period." *Furor scribendi.* That was our secret password. *(Wistfully.)* Such little things to so obsess our days and nights.

(She opens one book briefly, squints at the page, then closes it.)

We wove a web in childhood,
A web of sunny air;
We dug a spring in infancy
Of water pure and fair;

We sowed in youth a mustard seed,
We cut an almond rod;
We are now grown to riper age—
Are they withered in the sod?

The mustard seed in distant land
Bends down a mighty tree,
The dry, unbudding almond wand
Has touched eternity.

*(A clap of thunder interrupts the mood. CHARLOTTE returns
the little books to the shelf. She removes an ivory fan and
opens it.)*

Here's the ivory fan that Aunt Branwell gave Emily in her
will. Aunt Elizabeth Branwell was Mamma's sister. Brany was
named for her. Auntie came to live with us from Penzance in
Cornwall the May before Mamma died, and she never returned
to Penzance. *(Pause.)* Auntie enjoyed arguing fiercely with
Papa.

(As AUNTIE.) No, no, no, no, no, no, no, Mister Brontë!
I'm sure you're wrong. *(To audience.)* She always won.

(As TABBY.) A bit of a tyke, she wur—*(To audience:)*—
that's what Tabby says about Auntie—*(As TABBY.)* So crosslike
an' fault-findin'. An' so stingy. She ga'e us, Sally an' me, but
a gill o' beer a day, an' she ga'e it to us hersel', did Miss
Branwell. She wouldna let us go t'draw it oursel' in t'cellar.
No. Only a pint a day, she ga'e us. An' that wur half a pint for
me an' half a pint for Sally. Hmph!

With Calvinish fervor, Aunt Branwell taught us joyless re-
ligion and workaday sewing, neither of which Emily excelled
in. Her sampler is a horror. Brany embroidered the prettiest
one.

(She replaces the fan and picks up BRANY's sampler.)

Look at these French knots. And have you ever seen more perfect lazy daisies? Brany, I think, should've been a girl. He might have been happier.

(She finds AUNTIE's snuff box.)

Oh, Auntie's snuff box. *(Imitating AUNTIE taking snuff.)* "No, no, no, no, no, no, no, children, we do not use the word *spit*," she would say, with her little curls bouncing. "Never the word *spit*. If you must refer to the unpleasant discharging of unwanted matter from your chest cavity, you will hereafter use the word *expectorate*. Now repeat after me."

(She executes a prolonged sneeze.)

"Ex-pec-to-rate."

Oh, Auntie, in your black silk gown and lace mob cap, decreeing the rigid domestic schedule of our lives. Did you know that we cared for you? Did we ever tell you? Or thank you for giving up your plans, whatever they might have been, in sunny warm Penzance—to become mistress in this somber place?

And did you know that Brany doted on those false auburn curls so primly attached to your dear gray head? Oh, yes, Auntie, we knew that those springy curls were false. Brany secretly schemed to one night steal them while you slept, and pin them to Flossy's tail. Well, of course, he never did. Even the Duke of Wellington wouldn't have dared such an exploit. *(Regretfully.)* Oh, Auntie.

(We hear thunder and the sound of rain driving against the window. CHARLOTTE returns the snuff box to the cupboard.)

(To audience:) Like a North Pole day it is.

(In her mind, she resumes her letter.)

(To NELL:) Riding up from Keighley, Nell, the sky looked like ice. England might really have taken a slide up into the Arctic Zone, as some say.

(More thunder. She crosses and sits in the rocker, calling to MARTHA, offstage.)

Martha! Are the dogs inside? *(To audience:)* Flossy and Keeper are terrified of thunder. Flossy is Anne's dog—*was* Anne's dog. Keeper is a mastiff. Keeper followed Emily's coffin to the church. Now he spends most of each day lying outside her bedroom door upstairs.

(To MARTHA:) Let them come into the kitchen. They can sleep by the fire. Oh, and if it's all the same to you, I'd just as soon use the blue and white teapot after this. *(Pause.)* I know it was my aunt's, but I prefer the blue and white.

(To audience:) She's Martha Brown, the sexton's daughter. Martha's been with us since she was eleven. She came to help Tabby. Tabby has relinquished most of her exclusive tasks to Martha—with some jealous reluctance, I dare say. But they've always gotten on well.

Tabby was born in the year of our Lord only knows when. She must be eighty by now. She came to us a widow, when I was six. Tabitha Ackroyd. You saw she's lame? Well, last winter she fell at the top of Main Street, in front of the Black Bull Tavern. It's so steep there, don't you know, and the cobblestones were icy.

Our chief concern with Tabby is that she expects to be informed of all the family business. Yet, she's so deaf, I have to shout at her. And if Sally Mosley hears—Sally comes in to do the washing—if Sally hears, then the whole village knows. Sally is an incessant and most indiscreet talker. She's a good girl, but if her hands worked as fast as her mouth, she'd be the best laundress in England.

So, when I have something to tell Tabby, I take her out for a short walk on the moors behind the house—weather permitting—oh, just far enough so we can sit down in some secluded spot.

(She walks downstage and arranges two chairs, sitting in one.)

"Now, Tabby," I say, "what in God's name is so important?

And Tabby, puffing and blowing after the walk, and with much mincing and munching, says, "Oh, Miss Charlotte, Aw've heerd sich news!"

"What news?"

And then Tabby becomes very mysterious, and she says, "Agnes Wilberforce, t'Postmaster's wife down in Keighley, is noisin' it about that ya're after callin' yar'sel' Currier Bell, Esquire. An' she say ya've gone an' written that Jane Eyre tale, t'grandest tale that wur ever heerd. I do know ya're turrible larn'd, Miss Charlotte. Is it true?"

(Sighing, to TABBY:) Yes, Tabby, it's true. And it's not Currier, it's Currer. Currer Bell, Esquire. Agnes Wilberforce never could get things straight.

(As TABBY, cupping ear.) Hey? *(To TABBY, shouting:)* I say, it's true! But you must hold your tongue about it! And don't talk to Sally! *(As TABBY.)* Hey?

(To audience:) You see how difficult it is? Now, this all concerns the fact that when we decided to publish—Emily, Anne and I—we didn't want to declare ourselves women. We had some vague impression that authoresses were liable to be looked on with prejudice. So we decided to veil our names under those of Currer Bell for me, Ellis Bell for Emily, and Acton Bell for Anne. You see? The name Bell—*(Coyly.)*—well, we might have borrowed it from Mister Nicholls. It's his middle name.

It seemed a splendid joke—each of us with a published novel. Emily's "Wuthering Heights," Anne's book, "Agnes Grey" ...

(Picking up a book from the table.)

... and my "Jane Eyre." Mister Smith gave me this copy. It was the first one printed. *(Pause.)* Mister George Smith of Smith, Elder and Company. My publisher. Mister Smith wrote to me last summer, very concerned over the rumors that our three books were the product of one author. So Anne and I went up to London by train, with the view of proving our separate identities to Mister Smith. Emily didn't go, of course. She hardly ever ventured into society.

(She gets a letter from the cupboard.)

(Gleefully.) Mister Smith didn't know we were coming. He'd never seen us. He didn't know we were women. He'd always written to me as a man by the name of Currer Bell. So

I said, "Mister Smith, I present this letter as proof of my identity. It is addressed by you to Currer Bell, Esquire." "How did you come by it?" he asked. *(To SMITH:)* "It is addressed to me, sir. Mister Smith, mystery to me is irksome, and it is my wish to show myself to you for what I am, neither more nor less; thus removing any false expectation that Currer Bell has a just claim to the masculine cognomen, which he perhaps presumptuously adopted.

(Tangled in her words.) What I'm trying to say is—we've both come, sir, that you might have ocular proof that there are at least two of us. Wuthering Heights stayed at home.

(With impressive gravity.) Mister Smith, may I present— Acton Bell. *(To ANNE, whispering:)* Anne, that's you! *(To SMITH:)* And I, sir, am Currer Bell, Esquire.

(She curtsies low, then replaces her cloak, bonnet and letter.)

(To audience:) Our Postmaster, Samuel Feather, never once has asked about the three strange Bell brothers who receive mail at the Parsonage. But down at Keighley, where the mail is sorted—well, that's a different story. It seems a letter from my publisher was opened and read there by a certain someone, and her initials are A.W.! *(Whispering.)* Agnes Wilberforce.

(She finds the letter in question, and holds it from her with a look of disgust.)

The letter arrived here days later, crudely resealed and covered with purple smudges. Just look at that! Isn't that disgraceful? It seems Agnes Wilberforce was cooking beets that day. I understand her culinary pièce de résistance is beets and deviled kidneys. It's no secret why her family prays before every meal. With Agnes knowing about me, there'll be no more secrecy, you can be sure.

Last autumn, I finally had to tell Papa about my having written "Jane Eyre," what with all the talk, and strangers poking about.

"Excuse me, Papa," I said, "I'm sorry to disturb you, but I have something to tell you." *(As PAPA yawning.)* Have you, my dear? *(To PAPA:)* Yes—uh—Papa—I've written a book, and I want you to read it. *(As PAPA.)* No, Charlotte. I'm afraid it will try my old eyes too much. Your handwriting is so diminutive. *(To PAPA:)* But, Papa, my book isn't in manuscript. It's been printed.

(To audience:) And then you should have heard him! He was out of the chair like a shot. *(As PAPA.)* Charlotte Brontë! Have you incurred the expense of printing your own book, without asking your father's advice? It will almost certainly be a loss, you know that. How can a woman get a book sold? Besides, no one knows you. No one has ever heard of Charlotte Brontë. And let us not forget the folly of you and your sisters in printing that book of poems, which sold how many copies?

(To PAPA:) Oh, Papa. *(As PAPA.)* How many? *(To PAPA:)* Well, two copies, but—*(As PAPA.)* Two copies sold! No, my dear, I'm afraid you've raised your hopes too high this time. Remember, Charlotte, you are no Currer Bell. And your book, I think most certainly, will be no "Jane Eyre." *(To PAPA:)* But, Papa, that's what I've been trying to tell you. I *am* Currer Bell, and I've written "Jane Eyre!" *(Pause.)* Papa?

(CHARLOTTE imitates PAPA's snoring.)

(To audience.) I think Papa was proud when he woke up an hour later and realized he hadn't dreamed it. He told Emily and Anne, "Girls, do you know our Charlotte has been writing a book and it's much better than likely?" *(Laughing.)* Much better than likely. Whatever do you think he meant? But I do wish he'd stop harping about our poetry book. "Only two copies sold," he keeps saying. Papa dwells on failure. It's his staff and rod.

(She finds the poetry volume and examines it.)

It's not an unattractive volume. Yet, Anne and I both knew in our hearts that Emily's poetry was its one distinguishing feature.

(Opening the book, reading.)

No coward soul is mine,
No trembler in the world's storm-troubled sphere:
I see Heaven's glories shine,
And faith shines equal, arming me from fear.

Though earth and man were gone,
And suns and universes ceased to be,
And Thou were left alone,
Every existence would exist in Thee.

There is not room for Death,
Nor atom that his might could render void:
Thou—THOU art Being and Breath,
And what THOU art may never be destroyed.

(Closing the book.) As for our published novels—you know, my brother Brany never knew about them? He died not know-

ing. Well, in his condition of self-pity and dissipation—I ask you, how could we have told him?

(She sits in the rocker.)

I'm sorry. It's just that his life was such a tragic waste. (Pause.) This old rocker was Mamma's. It was one of her few possessions to be salvaged from a shipwreck on the way to Liverpool. That was before she married Papa. She died when I was five. It's a nice old chair.

(Pensively.) So fine and small he was. Brany, I mean. And wanting so desperately to be accepted, trying to be a swilling, swaggering little man among those crude brawlers at the Black Bull.

And he also—now, this will shock you—he also became addicted to opium. When we were in church, he'd steal down to the village druggist and cajole Betty Hardacre into giving him more of the drug. I'd often lie awake in the dead of night, listening, waiting, for the report of a pistol.

Perhaps I hoped he'd end his misery—or ours. He slept in Papa's room. We'd often hear him having delirium tremens of the most frightful character. Finally, I could endure it no longer.

"Branwell!" I said. "Can't you see what you're doing to Papa? Your moping gloom has spread a pall over this house. You think of nothing but stunning yourself with opiates and drowning yourself in rum. You, who had such promise.

"Well, I'll tell you this! I have for too long blinded myself to the magnitude of your failings. I'd hoped for your redemption. But, by God, hope in your case seems utterly wasted. Let

Emily leave the light burning for you, if she wants, so you can grope your way home every night. Let her leave the door unlatched. I would lock you out. I would never have believed I could utter such words—*but I am done with you!*"

(Stunned by her own vehemence.)

(To audience:) One Sunday morning—this past September twenty-fourth—Brany died. He was perfectly conscious to the end. His mind had undergone that peculiar change which frequently precedes death. A return of natural affections. An inner calm.

He's in God's hands now, and the All-powerful is likewise the All-merciful. A deep conviction that he rests at last, rests well after his brief, erring, suffering, feverish life—fills and quiets my soul. All his vices are nothing now. Nothing. Strange, isn't it? Till the last hour comes, we never know how much we can forgive.

(She takes a small box from a shelf and opens it.)

(Tenderly.) This was Brany's when he was a little boy. His collection of—shells? No. Coins? No. Stones? No. Marbles? No. Stamps? No. Buttons? No. *(Pause.)* Feathers. *(Removing them one by one.)* This is a turkey's. Our Feast of Pentecost. And this is a wild duck's. Ambushed by Keeper. And here is a moor cock's. Felled by a stone from the sling of a heartless boy. Oh, and a pigeon's. Its neck broken. And this one—I should know it among a thousand. It's a lapwing's. A bonny bird, wheeling over our heads in the middle of the moor. It wanted to get back to its nest ...

(She blows the feather from her hand and watches it flutter to the floor.)

... for it saw the clouds touch the swells, and it felt rain coming.

(She stoops and picks it up.)

This feather was picked up from the heath. The bird was shot. We saw its nest in the winter, full of little skeletons. For every smallest thing, there is sadness.

(She gently places the feathers back in the box.)

As I look back now, I see what I found difficult to forgive in Brany. More than the dissipation, the self-abuse, was the fact that he intrigued with the wife of his invalid employer, at whose house he was a private tutor—and was dismissed for that reason.

Adultery. The one, the only temptation it was my fate to endure. And to see him partake where I was denied, yield to carnal bliss where I suffered the purgatory of rejection—filled me with such scorn, such resentment, that only his dying could free me. *(Whispering.)* Forgive me.

(She closes the box.)

My purgatory, yes. Monsieur Constantin Heger. Auntie had granted us a loan, Emily and me, that would enable us to attend the Pensionnat Heger in the Rue d'Isabelle in Brussels, Belgium. It was our plan to acquire mastery of French, with the hope of opening our own school right here in Haworth. We sailed to Brussels in February, 1842, and the following October, Auntie died, and we came home.

But I couldn't leave him. Against my conscience, I returned

alone to Brussels. Against all conscience, all reason, prompted by the irresistible impulse of—what? Infatuation? Love? I don't know.

All I've ever wanted in life was love, a gentle time, a quiet time. Yet I know now that without esteem, love can't exist. It perishes for neglect. Pity may take its place, but pity is not love. And so, I returned to Brussels, and to Monsieur Heger. It was like a summons to resurrection.

Constantin Heger, professor of rhetoric. A man of great mental power. Discomposing chameleon eyes and dark brows. In the core of his heart was a place, tender beyond man's tenderness. But he could make me cry as no other man has, before or since.

My Black Swan.

He loaned me books, conversed with me—en français. I gave him English lessons. He gave me small presents. I was transformed in my own eyes. No longer plain, ugly little Charlotte Brontë ...

(A graceful Parisian waltz is heard briefly.)

... but youthful, fair, brilliant, whirling with him through the waltz, leaning on his arm in some green and sunny park, as he carried my parasol.

(To HEGER, adoringly:) Monsieur, if I could believe I please you, I could be at rest. I wouldn't be sad. If you withdraw your friendship from me entirely, I shall be altogether without hope. If you give me a little friendship, un petit peu, I shall be satisfied. *(Pleadingly.)* Monsieur, the poor have not

need of much to sustain them. They ask only for the crumbs that fall from the rich man's table.

You will tell me, perhaps, "I take not the slightest interest in you, Mademoiselle Charlotte—I shall forget you."

(To HEGER.) Ah, Monsieur, then tell me so frankly. It will be a shock to me. It matters not. It will be less dreadful than this uncertainty, this—que se—doute?

(Distant cathedral bells are heard briefly.)

My world came to a stop, when the school holiday began in August. The students all went home. Monsieur left for the seaside at Blankenburg. And for five weeks, I was alone in the desolate confines of the Pensionnat.

One evening, desperate and tormented, I left the house and, threading the streets of the neighborhood, I heard the bells of a church. I listened. The sound sailed full and liquid into my soul. It was the Cathedral of Sainte Gudule, and it was the hour of evening salut.

(A stained glass effect fades in across the floor of the stage. A voix celeste of a pipe organ whispers in the background.)

I went in and knelt down on the stone floor with the others. Only a few women were saying their prayers. In a solitary part of the cathedral, six or seven waited to confess. I didn't stir. I couldn't leave the church. Something held me there. After a space, a penitent approached the confessional. I watched. She whispered to a priest through a grating. And then another went, and another.

(Kneeling.) As if in a dream, I approached the confessional. I knelt down in the niche, trembling. A little door inside the grating opened. And I saw the white-haired priest leaning his ear toward me.

(She begins to weep.)

(To PRIEST:) I don't know the right words, mon père. I'm Protestant. There's no one else I can turn to. Please, Father, hear me. I'm perishing for advice. There's a weary weight on my heart that must be lifted. It's someone I love. I yearn to be near him. Only he is kind to me. Only he smiles at me. He's the one, the only one, worthy of being loved. It hurts to say good-bye to him, even for a day. Please, Father, my internal struggle is unbearable. I can't leave him. His slightest word of kindness I hold onto, as I hold onto life.

(She blows her nose, now more controlled and composed.)

Matrimony is out of the question.

(She rises abruptly, having had her fill of Catholicism.)

It's out of the question, that's all!

(Light returns to normal.)

(To audience:) Monsieur had a wife and three children, with a fourth on the way. In fact, my earliest recollection on arriving in Brussels is that of Madame Heger bending over, bustle askew, her eye glued to the keyhole of a classroom—not easy to do when you're eight months pregnant—watching her husband teach rhetoric to twenty-two dreamy-eyed young women.

It was obvious that Madame wanted me away from Brussels. She grew cold and distant. And yet, I waited for some sign from him. But none was given. The agony of time was stupefying. The monotony.

Then one day in the hall—*(To MADAME:)* Excusez moi, Madame, s'il vous plaît! Je donne notice. Je dois resigner. *(Pause.)* Oui, Madame. Je vous donne ma démission. A partir l'école ce jour! *(To audience:)* I resigned. And she promptly accepted my resignation. *(To herself:)* Oh, dear God, what have I done?

(To audience:) When Monsieur heard of it, he was in a fine rage. Well, at least I had *that* to cling to. Yet, it was Madame who saw me sail from Ostend. Oh, she wanted to be sure I was on that packet and out of their lives for good.

She authorized correspondence, all right. Until I wrote him a letter that was less than reasonable, because passion was at my heart. "I have tried to forget you, Monsieur, but I cannot. Fever claims me. I lose appetite and sleep. I pine away. I suffer in silence." *(Pause.)* I wore out my French dictionary. After that, there was nothing.

(To HEGER, agonized:) Oh, please, Monsieur, send me a letter. A letter from Brussels. Write it, Monsieur, write it, write it! But not out of pity, for that would wound me deeply. I fear by the mere asking—I offend you. But in my prideless obsession, I wish it all the same. Write it, Monsieur. A letter, a word.

(To audience:) Nothing more. Strange, obstinate grief. What a bourgeois, silly creature I was, with passions like convulsion fits. All that twaddle over a married man. *Twaddle.*

I understand from Laetitia Wheelwright, who has been in Brussels, that in these seven years, Monsieur's family has increased considerably. Laetitia says when the Heger children are in the yard, it looks like recess.

It's such an unfair state of things between men and the virgin population. The match isn't equal. Men can with impunity make a teasing pastime of our torments. So I say, Go to the deuce, Monsieur! *(Quietly.)* But may God protect you with special care, and crown you with peculiar blessings.

(There is a knock at the door. She listens.)

(To MARTHA offstage:) Who is it, Martha? Is it Mister Nicholls? *(Pause.)* Oh. Sally Mosley. *(To audience:)* With the altar cloth for Sunday. *(Calling out.)* Thank you, Sally! *(To herself:)* Maybe Mister Nicholls changed his mind about calling.

(She returns to her letter, putting on her spectacles.)

(To NELL:) This I have learned, Nell—you hold out your hand for a pearl, and Fate puts into it a scorpion. Show no consternation. Close your fingers firmly upon the gift. Let it sting through your palm. Never mind. In time, after your hand and arm have swelled and quivered long with torture, the squeezed scorpion will die, and you will have learned the great lesson of how to endure without a sob.

(To MARTHA offstage:) What is it? *(To audience:)* The potatoes. *(To MARTHA:)* Are you sure Tabby's asleep? *(To audience:)* Excuse me, I have an errand in the kitchen, a

secret mission. When I return, I'll tell you all about the *potatoes*!

(She exits.)

END OF ACT I

ACT II

*(SCENE: The stage is the same. The following is a continua-
tion of Act I.*
*AT RISE: CHARLOTTE enters furtively, carrying a bowl of
peeled potatoes and a paring knife.)*

CHARLOTTE. *(To audience:)* Remember, I said I'd tell
you about the potatoes? I won't tell you, I'll show you. I hope
Tabby didn't see me take this. You see, she reserves to herself
the right of peeling potatoes. *(As TABBY.)* Poilin' potatoes.

(To audience:) But she's practically blind, and she leaves
in these black specks—the eyes of the potato, we call them
here in the North. We can't bear to hurt her feelings by asking
Martha to go over them a second time. So, after Tabby has
pared them, we carry them off, without her knowing. And I
just take out these little black dots ...

*(She sits down and begins the task of removing the eyes from
the potatoes.)*

... like this, and Martha puts the bowl back in place. Tabby
never knows the difference. She's usually dozing by the kitchen

35

fire, anyway. *(Pause.)* Potatoes for tomorrow's soup.

(Sighing.) I'm afraid the life of a country parson's plain daughter with sunken eyes and sallow skin—and just a mention of a tic—is rooted in monotony. I have to laugh when I think of Nell's last letter. *(Imitating NELL.)* "Write soon, Charlotte, and tell me all the exciting news!"

(As she peels, she continues her letter to NELL.)

(To NELL:) What would you have me say, Nell? That Haworth's glittering social season was launched this weekend last in the Black Bull Tap Room, when Charlie Murgatroyd struck Matthew Pickles in the face and made his nose bleed? Or that Frank and Bessie Winkler are rejoicing over the birth of a new baby? *(Pause.)* Their seventeenth, to be exact. Are these happenings that whet your interest, Nell?

Or maybe that I have a miserable toothache? Or that my youth is gone, and will never come back? *(To audience:)* I'm sorry, but Haworth is drab. *(To FLOSSY:)* Flossy, stop your scratching, or out you go! *(To audience:)* London has its opera season and Haworth has its flea season.

Actually, I've seen so little of the world. Oh, I've been to London and, of course, Brussels. But before that, only short distances from this black magnet of a town.

I was bundled off to the Cowan Bridge School for the daughters of poor clergymen, when I was eight. Do you know the place? *(Pause.)* No, it's near Tunstall, Lancashire. My eldest sisters, Maria and Elizabeth, perished under the appalling negligence of the school at ten and twelve.

Miss Andrews, sadistic, sarcastic, cold-blooded, threw Maria to the dormitory floor once in a rage. Poor Maria. She had an open blister on her side. One morning she was too weak to get up when the bell rang. Miss Andrews said, "Well, m'lady, are we going to spend the day sleeping?" She jerked her out of bed and flung her down. I saw her do it! Oh, how I hated that creature!

(She stops paring potatoes.)

I'm a hearty hater, make no mistake. An avenging sister. There's an old saying in Yorkshire: "Keep a stone in thy pocket seven year; turn it, keep it seven year longer, that it may be ready to thine hand when thine enemy draws near." *(Impatiently.)* Oh, I know, I know! You'll say, "But the Bible tells us to return good for evil." Well, that's all very well. But I believe that when we're struck at without any reason, we should strike back again, *very hard.*

(She pounds her fist on the table.)

I'm sure we should. So hard as to teach the person who struck us never to do it again.

(She picks up her copy of "Jane Eyre.")

And I've struck back hard with this, for "Jane Eyre" brought to public notice the degrading regime of that institution. I've named the Cowan Bridge the Lowood School. Miss Andrews is now—*(To audience member:)*—Oh, yes? You've read it! Miss Andrews is now Miss Scatcherd. And the Reverend Karas Wilson, head of Cowan Bridge—that black pillar—has become the pompous Mister Brocklehurst. *(Perusing book for several beats.)* This is very good.

Oh, there's been consternation, you may be sure, from the patrons of the school and its founder. Well, so be it. If nothing else, "Jane Eyre" delivered me from a life of servitude. I speak of being a governess, a career for which I had no natural talent.

Take the Sidgwick household, for instance. The children were perfect little brats. I grew tired of tying their shoelaces and wiping their smutty little noses. John Benson, their four-year-old imp, even threw a Bible at me. The family Bible. When he saw I wasn't going to tattle on him, he said, "I love 'ou, Miss Bontë."

(Sniffle.)

Mrs. Sidgwick, whose over-sized ears heard everything, replied, "What? Love the governess? Ha, ha, ha, ha! Leave us hear no more such twiddle-twaddle, young man."

(Holding up potato and examining it.)

Sarah Sidgwick, with her vindictive black looks, Gorgon-like face, pointed head ...

(Cutting two lines in potato with paring knife.)

... and little black moustache. *(Pause.)* Have you studied phrenology? You know—the study of the cranium as an indication of intelligence? Well, I'm sure Mrs. Sidgwick's extraction must have been low. She used abominable grammar and worse orthography. She thought syntax was the money collected by the church from sinners. Incredible.

I think I'd rather work in a mill than be a governess. The chief requisite for that station seems to me to be the power of taking things easily as they come, a quality in which all Brontës are deficient.

(She rises, finished with the potatoes, and places the bowl on a table, over which hangs the Hero painting.)

There. *(Pointing to picture.)* Oh, do you see this? Emily did it.

(Squinting at the picture, her nose almost touching it, she reads with difficulty.)

"October 27th, 1841." There, you see? I don't need spectacles. I can see perfectly well without them. It's a painting of Hero, a beautiful hawk that Emily rescued out on the moors. It was tiny and abandoned.

We had many pets. Two geese, Adelaide and Victoria, named after Adelaide, regnant queen to William the Fourth; and, of course, Her Royal Highness, Queen Victoria. They slept in the peat room on some old rags. *(Pause.)* The geese, I mean.

(CHARLOTTE pours tea. She glares at the teapot.)

I do wish Martha would use the blue and white teapot. This one was Auntie's, and I'm quite put off by the quotation on it: "To me to live is Christ, to die is gain."

To die is gain?

It was William Grimshaw's favorite text. *(Pause.)* Oh— William Grimshaw. You've not heard of him? Saint Michael

and All Angels was Mister Grimshaw's church long before
Papa became its pastor.

You're not Catholic, are you? Mister Grimshaw was less
than tolerant of Catholics. "Brimstone Grimshaw," Brany used
to call him. They still tell the story of how, one Sunday morning, the Reverend flogged the sinners out of the Black Bull
Tavern with a horse-whip, and into the church.

*(CHARLOTTE puts down the teacup daintily and takes up the
broom, flailing it about and advancing across the stage
menacingly in imitation of GRIMSHAW.)*

(As GRIMSHAW.) Get ye into the House of the Lord, ye
foul, besmirched, miserable, back-sliding, sin-ridden sons of
Satan! *Crack!* Crawl in supplication on your knees! Repent
before the wrath of the Lord, or be thrown into the everlasting
fires of Hell, from whence no man may ever be delivered, but
must burn and burn and burn in the eternal flames of God's
wrath! Crack! Vile, disobedient offspring of Beelzebub!
Winebibbers, fornicators! Your transgressions are legion, and
your days are numbered! Now drag your lustful, bloated bodies into the Temple of the vengeful Jehovah and cast your loath-
some eyes down in shame and supplication before the feet of
your Lord and Savior, Jesus Christ, who will smite you with
the rod of correction, even as I do this day! Repent! Repent,
or die!

(She pauses, hearing PAPA from the other room.)

(To PAPA:) No, Papa! I'm fine!

(She puts the broom back and sits down in the rocker.)

(To audience:) Poor Brimstone Grimshaw, entirely convinced of his own pristine righteousness. Brow-beating and body-beating his victims into the kingdom of heaven, or into what he thought was heaven. *(Studying teapot.)* "To die is gain." Saint Paul's words.

Mister Grimshaw revered Paul. Well, they were birds of a feather, that's why. Mister Grimshaw even had the motto painted on the sounding board above the pulpit. "To die is gain." It's still there, hanging over Papa's head every Sunday morning, like an archangel's cleaver.

And Mister Grimshaw had the saying preached at his funeral and inscribed on his coffin. Such a strange motto for a life. "To die is gain." *(Pause.)* Well, maybe in a way it was gain when he died. At least, for the customers at the Black Bull. *(Pause.)* Such a morbid little teapot.

(She rises and gets a lamp from the mantle.)

The daylight is almost gone. You'd never know it turned summer today. Yorkshire is a place apart, that's God's truth.

(The front door knocker sounds. CHARLOTTE freezes for a moment. She moves across the stage quietly, listening. Then she shrugs and turns away.)

(To herself:) Joseph Redman to see Papa. Why did Mister Nicholls ask if he could call, if he had no intention of doing so?

(She goes to the fire, lights a taper, and returns to light the lamp.)

Why is my hand trembling so? Like that of an old man.

(She succeeds in lighting the lamp, then blows out the straw.)

There. Burn, little lamp. Burn straight and clear.

(She picks up the mask from the mantle.)

(To audience:) Oh, I haven't shown you this. Papa bought this in Thornton when we were very small. It's made of papier-mâché. You hold it like this. Papa suspected we children knew more than we expressed, and he thought if we could speak incognito, we'd have less inhibitions.

"Who wants to be first?" he asked. And after some giggling and scuffling of feet, little Anne stepped forward. "Me," she said bravely.

(As PAPA:) All right, put the mask over your face. Now you're not little Anne Brontë anymore. You're anyone you wish to be. What's your name? *(As ANNE, with mask.)* Anne Brontë. *(As PAPA.)* But don't you want to be someone else? *(As ANNE, with mask.)* No, I like me. *(As PAPA.)* Very well, Anne Brontë, what does a four-year-old child like you want most in this world? *(As ANNE, with mask.)* Age and experience. *(As PAPA.)* Age and experience! A wise choice. Precisely what you lack, my girl. Now give the mask to Emily.

(As PAPA to EMILY.) And what's your name, my good woman? *(EMILY, with mask.)* On your knees, vassal slave! I am Queen Augusta. *(As PAPA.)* A queen at six years? *(As EMILY, with mask.)* A beautiful queen, who feeds her vanity on the souls of men. *(As PAPA.)* Yes, your Highness. Now tell me, what had I best do with your brother Branwell when

he is naughty? *(As EMILY, with mask.)* Branwell? Who is Branwell? We have no kin by that name. But had We, We would reason with him, and if he wouldn't listen to reason, We'd have him whipped by Our Royal Henchmen. *(As PAPA.)* Thank you, your Majesty.

(As PAPA to BRANWELL.) Now, Brany, it's your turn. Come over here, lad, and stop hiding. Now, what distinguished name do *you* bear, sir? You have the mask upside down, lad. *(As BRANWELL, with mask.)* Oh—my name is Patrick Benjamin Wiggins, at your service, sir. *(As PAPA.)* How old are you, Mister Wiggins? *(As BRANWELL with mask.)* Seven years. *(As PAPA.)* Do you have any relatives? *(As BRANWELL, with mask.)* Oh, I've some people who call themselves akin to me in the shape of three girls. They are honored by possessing me as a brother, but I deny that they're my sisters. *(As PAPA.)* What are their names? *(As BRANWELL, with mask.)* Charlotte Wiggins, Emily Wiggins, and Anne Wiggins. *(As PAPA.)* And are they as queer as you? *(As BRANWELL, with mask.)* Oh, Charlotte's a dumpy little thing. Emily's face is the size of a penny. And Anne is nothing, absolutely nothing. *(As PAPA.)* What? Is she an idiot? *(As BRANWELL, with mask.)* Well, next door to it. *(As PAPA.)* Well, Mister Wiggins, what do you think is the best way of knowing the difference between the intellects of men and women? *(As BRANWELL, with mask.)* Well, you must look at how they are different in their bodies. *(As PAPA.)* What do you mean, sir? *(As BRANWELL, with mask.)* I mean, women being softer and smaller, their minds must be so, too. *(As PAPA.)* I see. That's a most interesting theory.

(As PAPA to CHARLOTTE.) And now, Charlotte. *(As herself.)* Yes, Papa. *(As PAPA.)* What's the best book in the world? *(As herself, with mask.)* You make sport with me, sir.

The Bible, of course, I commend it to all my subjects. *(As PAPA.)* Not another queen? *(As herself, with mask.)* An empress. *(As PAPA.)* Well, your Grace, what do you think is the next best book to the Bible? *(As herself, with mask.)* The Book of Nature, of course. Why do you bother me with these childish questions? I command you to begone!

(She lowers the mask slowly.)

(To audience:) This mask. How many times I've wished for a new visage between the world and Charlotte. I don't mean merely a name—Currer Bell, Esquire. I mean a total mask to hide old imperfections and to give a recreated self, inside and out.

Sometimes the future terrifies me. What's to become of Charlotte Brontë? What's to become of Currer Bell? Which taskmaster should I serve? Where is the end to this maze of turnings, to this isolation? Were it in my power, I would command—*(lifting mask to her face)*—a gentle time, a quiet time.

(She sits at the table, puts on her spectacles, and resumes her letter to NELL.)

(To NELL:) I suppose, Nell, life at the Parsonage will resume its full and vacant pattern, and care of Papa will be my chief concern in life now, to the exclusion of writing. Should he get better, I think I could rally and become Currer Bell once more. But if otherwise, I look no further than completing my present work and doing no more.

(To audience:) Men are strange creatures. I'm sorry, but they are. Helpless, really. Papa now has me only—the weakest, puniest, least promising of all his six children. And yet, he tells me this day, "Be strong, Charlotte, or I am lost."

I think Papa became lost when Mamma died. Her last words were, "Oh, God, my poor children." She was buried under the stones at the east end of the church. And then, our lives grew lonelier still.

(She crosses to a picture of her mother.)

I've tried very hard in the years since to summon up an image of my mother. The impressions of a child are so fragmentary, so elusive. And this picture doesn't remind me of anyone. I have only one recollection of Mamma. Once in the evening lamplight, when she played with Brany on the parlor floor. And it's her I remember more than Mamma.

Later that night, Emily and I heard Mamma singing to Brany from the nursery—

(Singing.) Sleep, my Brany, peace attend thee,
All through the night.
Guardian angels God will lend thee,
All through the night.

I'll never forget how Papa vented his anger and grief when she died—by firing his pistols out the back door in rapid succession. He'd had the pistols for protection ever since the Luddite riots. A pair of flint-lock pistols.

(Arms raised, as if firing into the sky.)

Up at the sky he fired. Tears were coursing down his face. He fired and fired and fired. "Why is Papa crying?" Brany asked. Well, he was frightened. He didn't understand. He was only four. "Why is Papa crying?"

Before I took Anne to Scarborough, an incident happened which curiously touched me. Papa put into my hand a little packet of letters, telling me they were Mamma's, and that I might read them.

(She lifts the lid of a box and removes a packet of letters, tied with a ribbon. She removes one.)

These were all written to Papa before their marriage. There's a rectitude, a refinement, a constancy, a modesty, a sense, a gentleness about them—indescribable. I wish Mamma had lived, and that I had known her.

(Reading aloud.) "My dear saucy Pat—I do not, cannot, doubt your love. And here I freely declare I do love you above all the world." *(To audience, wonderingly.)* Above all the world.

It's almost impossible for me to realize there lived a woman who cherished such sentiments for him. I've only known the man who never dresses in the morning without putting a loaded pistol in his pocket, as regularly as he puts on his watch. The little deadly pistol sits down to breakfast and kneels in prayer.

It seems "dear saucy Pat" is no more. I think he died when Mamma died. Now there's only a depleted old man who takes Original Sin for granted. On the surface—bland, kind. Underneath—hard as flint.

(She returns the letters to the box. Gusts of wind are heard. She listens.)

Sometimes the wind is so unremitting, wild, sweeping up and over our little house and down the hills.

(She puts on her shawl.)

Such a wind it was, the day of Brany's funeral. Emily took cold that day. She never went out of doors again. She sank rapidly. Never in all her life had she lingered over any task that lay before her, and she didn't linger then. She made haste to leave us. The deep, tight cough, the labored breathing after the least exertion.

(Sitting.) Many times, Anne and I dropped our sewing, or stopped writing, to look at each other and listen to the failing step and the long pauses, as Emily climbed the staircase. But we could say nothing. She rejected our help. We dared not speak a word of sympathy.

I finally sent for the doctor. He arrived, and she refused to see him. Refused. Anne and I could only describe to him what symptoms we had observed. And the medicines he sent, she refused to take. "I'm not ill," she declared, "and no poisoning doctor is going to come near me."

Moments so dark I've never known. Yet, while physically she perished, mentally she grew stronger than we had yet known her. I've seen nothing like it. Stronger than a man, simpler than a child, her nature stood alone.

(To EMILY:) Sister, you've sat there all the day,
Come to the hearth awhile;
The wind so wildly sweeps away,
The clouds so darkly pile.
That open book has lain, unread,
For hours upon your knee;
You've never smiled nor turned your head;
Sister, what can you see?

(As EMILY.) I'm on a distant journey bound,
And if, about my heart,
Too closely kindred ties were bound,
'Twould break when forced to part.
Ere long, nor sun nor storm to me
Will bring or joy or gloom;
They reach not that Eternity
Which soon will be my home.

(To audience:) It was a Tuesday morning this last December, I went searching the moors for a sprig of heather to bring to her. And when I found one, I ran all the way back home to lay it on her pillow. *(To EMILY:)* Emily! Emily, see what I found on the heights!

(To audience:) It filled me with such sadness to see her indifference to the flower she so dearly loved. But then she arose and dressed as usual, doing everything for herself, and weak as she was, even endeavoring to comb her hair. Tabby and Martha looked on with tears in their eyes. Well, all our hearts were breaking.

At two o'clock, when it was too late, she came down those stairs, lay down on that settee, and said to me, "Charlotte, if you'll send for the doctor, I'll see him now."

(She starts up.)

(To EMILY:) Yes! *(Turning.)* Emily ... ? *(To audience:)* And she died. *(To EMILY:)* Oh, God of Heaven! Emily, you were the nearest thing to my heart in all the world. "Mine bonny love," I used to call you. But there's no Emily in time or earth now. You're at peace. There's no need to tremble for the hard frost or keen wind. You don't feel them now.

(With resignation, she sits on the settee.)

(To audience:) We must never knit human ties too closely, or clasp our loved ones too fondly, because they must leave us, or we must leave them—one day. Papa and I are alone in the house. A suitable pair to divide the desolation between us. We've both suffered. Yet I don't suffer because I'm weak or that I can't exist without another to lean on, because I can.

But he can't. And so, I groan, not because I'm a single woman and likely to remain single. I groan because I'm a lonely woman and likely to remain lonely. I am solace for Papa, but he is not solace for me. But it can't be helped; therefore, it must be borne.

(To audience:) My friend from Roe Head School, Mary Taylor—we call her Pag—has emigrated to New Zealand to look for a new life. Brave girl. Pag writes that in the Wellington settlement, there are five hundred eligible redcoats to two hundred forty-eight spinsters. And Pag is personally acquainted with six grocers, one draper, two parsons, two clerks, two lawyers, and three or four nondescripts. All eligible.

(Figuring in her head.) Now, let's see. Five hundred redcoats, plus, say, a hundred eligible bachelors—that's a total of—six hundred—divided by two hundred forty-eight spinsters—carry the one—ten take away two leaves eight. *(Gasping.)* That's almost two and a half bachelors to one spinster!

Pag also writes that she knows a woman there with a glass eye and a wooden leg, who's had three husbands and nine children. Isn't it amazing? A wooden leg! Think of it!

Do you know, when I was fourteen, Pag told me I was ugly? She did. It was at Miss Wooler's Roe Head School, soon after I arrived. Miss Wooler made us good little girls learn how to be good little governesses.

Anyway, Emily didn't believe that anyone could say that I was ugly, especially Pag. "I'm sure you misunderstood her, Charlotte," Emily said. "You do exaggerate."

"Well, perhaps you're right," I said. "I'd certainly like to think so."

"Of course, I'm right," Emily assured me. "Now, tell me exactly, word for word, what Pag *really* said, and this time— don't embellish."

"Oh, all right," I said. "Her exact words were—(Pause.)— 'Charlotte Brontë, you're ugly.' "

I do notice that after any male stranger has once looked at my face, he's careful never to let his eyes wander to that part of the room again. Papa has a vehement antipathy to the bare thought of any man looking upon me as a possible wife. He calls it "that obnoxious subject." And quite frankly, I'm beginning to resent his attitude. I mean, what is so obnoxious about someone marrying me?

Why, if Papa fancies me the object of any gentleman's courtesy, he becomes absolutely hostile. The veins on his temples stand up like whipcord, and his eyes become bloodshot.

With every fresh tirade of his, my wretched liver becomes disordered again. Well, I suppose I must expect this derangement from time to time, living as I do with the most implacable old man in Yorkshire.

Papa has just gotten over his spring attack of bronchitis.
Next will be his summer attack of bronchitis. I trust it may
pass over in the comparatively ameliorated form in which it
has hitherto shown itself, so that he'll be strong enough to
greet his autumn attack of bronchitis with renewed zest.

Papa told me that if I marry and leave him, he'll "give up
housekeeping and go into lodgings," which is tantamount to
saying he'll lie down and die. It's precisely the meaning he
intends to convey.

As for "that obnoxious subject," I did have a proposal. Oh,
yes. I had no personal repugnance to the idea of union with
the gentleman. It's just that mine isn't the sort of disposition
calculated to make a man like Henry happy.

I speak of Nell's brother, Henry Nussey. He's the curate at
Bonnington. To put it bluntly, Henry bores me. Most clerics
do, but Henry bores me even when he's complimenting me.

Henry proposed by letter. I declined by letter. Not what
you would call a passionate courtship. I wrote to him, "Henry,
don't be downhearted. You will find a beautiful woman to
marry."

He wrote back, "I don't want a beautiful woman, Charlotte. I want you."

Generally, I detest clerics, with their petrified, proud looks.
All they can talk about is minute points of ecclesiastical disci-
pline—or food.

(She picks up a potato and studies it.)

This potato reminds me of Henry. It's precisely the shape of his head. Have you ever studied phrenology? Or did I ask you that?

Clerics seem to me a vain, self-seeking race. Except one— Willy Weightman. Willy was worth two hundred Henrys tied in a bunch. Willy. He came to Haworth in 1838 to assist Papa. Twenty-five years old, the son of a brewer in Appleby. Emily and Anne and I called him "Celia Amelia." Well, he was rather pretty, with his blushes and his bouncing curls. "Miss Celia Amelia Weightman," we called him. Willy didn't mind.

I'd say, "Good morning, your young Reverence," and his eyes would sparkle. He was cheery and good-tempered all the time, with a bonny face and a warm soul. Perfectly conscious of his irresistibleness, which made him all the more irresistible.

He danced with me once—a harmless little twirl around the kitchen. *(To WILLY:)* Oh, Willy, you take my breath away. *(To audience:)* Then Papa came in. *(To PAPA:)* Papa! *(To audience:)* "And what do you think you're doing, young woman?" he said. *(To PAPA:)* I'm dancing, Papa. *(As PAPA:)* You're a minister's daughter. *(To PAPA:)* Yes, which make me clumsier in the arms of a dancing partner than the daughter of a barrister. *(To audience:)* And Papa said, "I don't blame Mister Weightman. I blame you. Woman is again the seducer of man, this time under the sacred roof of my own parsonage. To think—my daughter allowing her body to be clasped in such a manner. I'm ashamed for you, prancing about the kitchen in such a ridiculous fashion." *(To PAPA:)* Ridiculous, Papa, only because I stepped on Mister Weightman's toes too many times. But I enjoyed the waltz immensely, and I shall very likely enjoy it again. *(As PAPA:)* The curse of Eve is on this place, God help us!

Celia Amelia. And Willy called me "Soul Divine." You see? Irresistible. But when he died of cholera in the 1842 epidemic, and even though it was Anne who secretly loved him, it was Brany who cried for days.

Three months ago, I came upon a poem of Brany's describing Willy—"lips that even me beguile." Oh, Brany. Strange, isn't it—love?

I don't know if—well, I don't know if I could ever love a man like Mister Nicholls. He's so reserved and grave. I respect him, but I don't like that dark religious gloom of his. I guess it's his narrow, sectarian views that offend me. He seems to always be wearing a sort of mental mackintosh. Do you know what I mean?

Of course, if I were to marry such a man—oh, what am I saying? *(Pause.)* But *were* I to marry such a man, I should never let him make me a bigot.

Mister Nicholls isn't what you'd call handsome, or even what is considered agreeable in outward aspect.

(Studying another potato.)

Actually, he's rather unappealing. *(Pause.)* But not altogether. I mean, not repulsive, certainly. But not comely, either. No, definitely not comely. *(Pause.)* Rather ill-featured, in fact. *(Pause.)* But he does have—kind eyes. Yes! That's it! Kind eyes. And—uh—*(Long pause.)*—well, kind eyes. And you might say—oh, no. No, you couldn't say that. Truthfully, I'd have to say that Mister Nicholls looks *cadaverous. (Tapping foot on floor.)* Well, he'll be right at home here.

(She puts on spectacles again, and resumes her letter.)

(To NELL:) I'm sure of it, Nell. Mister Nicholls cares for me. Yes, yes, he does. I've long suspected as much. He sometimes looks at me so fervently. ·

(CHARLOTTE is now deeply absorbed in a sense of romantic portent.)

When he bade me goodbye today, it dawned on me what might be coming. Oh, I know what Papa will say. "Arthur Bell Nicholls? Now I see it all. He plots to take you from me—the penniless schemer!"

(To PAPA:) Penniless he may be, Papa, but I don't consider him a schemer. Oh, Papa, no one plots to take me from you. I did not say I wish to leave here.

Papa, I'm not a young girl. I'm not a young woman, even. I never was pretty. Now I'm ugly. Oh, yes! And at your death, I shall have three hundred pounds, besides the little I've earned myself. Now, do you think there are many men who would serve four years for me, as Mister Nicholls has? I know I've ridiculed curates, but if I marry at all, I must marry a curate, and not just any curate, but your curate. And he must live in this house with you, for I cannot leave you.

(Firmly.) I'm sorry, Papa, but if Providence grants me this destiny, doubtless, then, it is best for me. And if this good man proposes marriage, I shall accept—*I shall accept*! And he will

live in this house—*(Relentlessly.)*—*He will live in this house,* and he will support you and console you in your old age. He'll help with the church and school, when you wish relief from them. And we'll both see that you maintain your seclusion uninvaded. *(With finality.)* You see Papa, I, too, am possessed of a stubborn will. *I am your daughter.*

(To audience:) And he'll grumble all the way up the stairs. *(As PAPA:)* "He won't ask her. It's only surmise, her woman's reckless, romantic imagination. He already suffers from rheumatic pains. Joseph Redman told me so. She'll have two invalids on her hands by and by, mark my words. Willful nonsense! A most obnoxious subject!" Grumble, grumble, grumble. *(To PAPA:)* Be careful on the stairs! And don't forget to wind the clock!

(To audience:) I could convert the peat room into a study for Mister Nicholls—that is, if he proposes. I think green and white curtains. And fresh wallpaper. *(Listening.)* How still it is outside, The wind, I think, has chased itself away.

(She sits at the table, puts on her spectacles and resumes her letter.)

(To NELL:) And so, dear Nell, Twilight is with me, and tranquil, ruddy Firelight. With these sisters, the Bright and the Dark, I will commune, as I write to you from this loneliest place on earth, where I fear the angels of God have abandoned me forever.

Oh, I'll wag on as usual. A little sour sometimes, perhaps. I was never known for sugariness. But as of today, I have a new creed—a belief in Happiness.

I've lived at the border of Death for a long time, heard the funeral bells tolling across the lane, listened to the "chip, chip" of the mason, as he cuts the tombstones in a shed close by. One by one, my earthly supports have been pulled away, until I'm alone with an old man who right now sleeps a fitful sleep.

(Removing her spectacles, still composing the letter in her mind.)

I mustn't fail him. I must stay on at the Parsonage. For Emily and Anne, For Branwell, for Maria and Beth, for Mamma, for Auntie. I'll run the house for Papa, teach in his Sunday School, read the Bible to him every night. And I'll do my duty without complaint, for I know that bitter are the upbraidings of my conscience, when I yield to a desire to flee this Heaven and Hell.

And if my new creed is true, then Happiness will find me. It will center my world at last, reawaken my heart. Of its aspect, I cannot speak, but it will find me. It will range the moors, like the summer rain. I will see it in the sun and sky. Its trace of glory will rest on the flowering heath. I shall wait and watch for its purple signal, listen for its whisper in the wind, its knock on the door—

(The door knocker sounds. CHARLOTTE turns, wild-eyed, excited.)

(To audience:) Remember the arch of today's rainbow? A perfect rainbow, wasn't it? Wide, high, vivid, spanning the moors. I must hope—it is my bow of promise!

(The knocker sounds again.)

(To MARTHA:) Martha, answer the door!

(She turns to finish the letter.)

(To NELL:) Come back to Haworth soon, Nell, but don't come in black. Come in blue, pink, white—even scarlet, for all I care. Come shabby or smart. Neither color nor condition signifies. Provided the dress contain my Nell, all will be right. C.B.

(To MARTHA, offstage, whispering:) Yes, Martha? *(Pause.)* No, I'll show him in.

(She turns back to the letter.)

(To NELL:) P.S. Oh, Nell, exciting news at last! Mister Nicholls waits in the hall! C.B. again.

(She removes her spectacles, picks up the mask and studies it.)

(As PAPA:) One more question, your Majesty. What do you most want in this world? *(To herself, pondering.)* What do I most want? *(With mask.)* A gentle time, a quiet time—I command.

(She puts down the mask and begins cross.)

(To NICHOLLS offstage:) Mister Nicholls—how good of you to call.

(As CHARLOTTE exits, Curtain Falls.)

END OF PLAY

PROPERTY LIST

<u>COSTUME</u>:
   Plain English dress for traveling, cloak, bonnet, gloves,
   shawl, spectacles, crocheted purse, all in style of 1840s.

<u>PARLOR FURNITURE</u>:
   Upholstered settee
   Small carved rocking chair
   Lamp table
   China cabinet
   Pianoforte, style of 1830s (optional)
   Large writing table
   Two chairs at table
   Coat tree
   Tea cart
   Umbrella stand

<u>FIREPLACE</u>:
   Peat
   Bellows
   Andirons
   Poker
   Small broom

<u>ACCESSORIES</u>:
   Large central rug, two smaller rugs
   Hatbox and carrying case
   Ink well, quill and paper
   Tea service (with cosy and inscribed teapot)
   Two hurricane lamps
   Several books of old binding
   Toy soldiers
   Tiny handmade books

Ivory fan
Mask with bells
Embroidered sampler
Snuff box
Packet of letters tied with ribbon
Letters in drawer
Lacquered box with feathers inside
Bowl of potatoes with paring knife

SET DESCRIPTION

The stage is raked downward from the back facade of the Brontë parlor, which includes a fireplace. This room is actually a dining room, but serves Charlotte Brontë as a sanctuary. For the action of the play, other elements of the Parsonage are consolidated in this room, which includes a small upholstered settee, a carved rocker, a china cabinet, a small lamp table, two hurricane lamps, a tea service, a bellows and small broom on the hearth, several framed pictures, and many books. The cabinet contains small objects, among which are wooden soldiers, an ivory fan, a belled mask and a lacquered box containing assorted feathers. A coat tree is partially visible.

While presenting the essence of a Victorian parlor, the set is not circumscribed in any conventional way. The feeling of the outside, the windswept moors and remote isolation of the Yorkshire high country, should pervade the stage.